SKY CASTLE

By Sandra Hanken

Illustrations by Jody Bergsma

ILLUMINATION Arts

PUBLISHING COMPANY, INC.

Bellevue, Washington

ILLUMINATION Arts

PUBLISHING COMPANY, INC.

P.O. Box 1865, Bellevue, WA 98009

Tel: 425-644-7185 * 888-210-8216 (orders only) * Fax: 425-644-9274

liteinfo@illumin.com * www.illumin.com

Library of Congress Cataloging-in-Publication Data

Hanken, Sandra, 1951–

    Sky castle / by Sandra Hanken ; illustrated by Jody Bergsma.

       p. cm.

    Summary: Fairies help to build a castle in the sky. Filled with hopes and dreams and imagination and rooms for all the animals of the world.

    ISBN 0-935699-14-7 (hardcover)

    [1. Castles--Fiction. 2. Animals--Fiction. 3. Fairies--Fiction. 4. Imagination--Fiction. 5. Stories in rhyme.] I. Bergsma, Jody, ill. II. Title.

PZ8.3.H1935Sk 1998

[E]--DC21
                                    98-17116

                                        CIP

                                        AC

3rd Printing

Published in the United States of America

Printed by Tien Wah Press in Singapore

Book Designer:

Molly Murrah, Murrah & Company, Kirkland, WA

Illumination Arts is a member of Publishers in Partnership – replanting our nation's forests.

Dedicated with love to my family – Larry, Brad, and Katie –
and to the dreamer inside all of us.

Sandra Hanken

Dedicated to the magic my parents, Les and Arden, bring to me.

Jody Bergsma

Inspire Every Child Foundation

A portion of the profits from this book will be donated to Inspire Every Child, a non-profit foundation dedicated to helping disadvantaged children around the world. This organization provides inspirational children's books to individuals and organizations that are directly involved in supporting the welfare of children. The directors and officers of Inspire Every Child provide their services on a voluntary basis, so donations go directly to help children in need. Your help in supporting this worthwhile cause would be greatly appreciated. Please visit **www.inspire-every-child.org** for more information.

Let's build a great castle high up in the sky.
We'll just close our eyes and let ourselves fly
To a bright new world of our own creation,
Full of hopes and dreams and imagination.

Climb rainbow stairs to the top of the sky.
Shout "Hello" to the Earth and feel her reply.
Then soar on the wind and reach toward the sun.
Our magical journey has now begun.

As we skip on the clouds, the heavens will sing.
Imagine a castle that's fit for a king.
Let's all work together, each adding our part
So it will be perfect right from the start.

The floors may be crystal or emerald or gold.
The doors can be new and the keys can be old.
Imagine great towers that stand for all time,
With spiraling staircases, tempting to climb.

Let's build our castle so high and so wide,
There'll even be room for whole oceans inside.
We'll swim with the dolphins, the turtles and whales,
And bounce on the waves in a boat with clear sails.

There'll be misty rain forests in tropical hues,
Hot deserts, vast prairies, high mountaintop views,
Clean rippling rivers and blue skies above,
All bright, clear and sparkling with sunshine and love.

We'll have room for the tigers and owls so wise,
For puppies and kittens and dragonflies.
Lions and zebras can lead the procession
Of animals coming from every direction.

There'll be icebergs for penguins and forests for bears,
Treetops for eagles and meadows for hares.
We'll have just the right homes for all of Earth's creatures.
This will be one of our castle's best features.

Let's fill up our castle with all of life's treasure,
Like warm hugs and smiles and love beyond measure.
Light hearts and laughter will start each new day,
To brighten our path and show us the way.

All will be welcome, our fathers and mothers,
Grandparents, neighbors, our sisters and brothers.
From farms, towns and cities, we'll walk hand in hand,
With all our new friends and hope from each land.

When at last it encircles the whole world 'round,
We'll bring our Sky Castle way down to the ground.
Let's slide it on moonbeams, with music and prayers,
Down to the Earth from our kingdom upstairs.

We'll set it down gently, with wisdom and care,
Then join as one family to celebrate there.
Let's all dance together, sing songs, and be free.
Imagine how wondrous our Earth Castle will be.

Now plan your creation, *your* dream in the sky.
No castle is built by those who don't try.
Remember, as long as you think and you feel,
Imagination and love will make *your* dream real.

Sandra Hanken

Though *Sky Castle* is the first book for Minnesota resident Sandra Hanken, she's no stranger to the world of children. She has been an elementary school teacher, a parenting educator, and is currently a family social worker.

For many years, Sandra aspired to write a book that would encourage children to believe in themselves and their abilities. One January night, she awoke with the words "Let's build a castle in the sky. We'll build a castle, you and I." When the rest of the poem came to her a few days later, she knew Jody Bergsma would be the perfect person to illustrate her story.

Surrounded by woods and wildlife, Sandra and her husband live in their country home near the town of Chisholm, Minnesota. They have two grown children.

Sandra Hanken

Jody Bergsma

Jody Bergsma

"I immediately knew I wanted to illustrate *Sky Castle* after receiving Sandra Hanken's inspiring poem," says Jody Bergsma. "Making dreams come true is a reoccurring theme in my paintings and my life." The daughter of a bush pilot father and a "very adventurous" mother, Jody believes her creativity springs largely from the richness and beauty of the world she experienced during her youth.

An internationally acclaimed artist, Jody lives near Bellingham, Washington. *Sky Castle* joins *Dreambirds, Dragon, The Little Wizard, Faerie,* and *The Right Touch* to form our award-winning Jody Bergsma Collection. For more information on Jody's original paintings, prints, and gift items call 1-800-BERGSMA or visit www.bergsma.com.

More inspiring picture books from Illumination Arts

Just Imagine
John M. Thompson & George M. Schultz/Wodin, ISBN 0-9740190-6-2
Ready for fun and adventure? Then join us in our magic tree house, where imagination takes flight as we blast off on the trip of a lifetime.

Am I a Color Too?
Heidi Cole/Nancy Vogl/Gerald Purnell, ISBN 0-9740190-5-4
A young interracial boy wonders why people are labeled by the color of their skin. Seeing that people dream, feel, sing, dance and love regardless of their color, he asks, "Am I a color, too?"

Mrs. Murphy's Marvelous Mansion
Emma Perry Roberts/Robert Rogalski, ISBN 0-9740190-4-6
During a tour of Mrs. Murphy's amazing home, her judgmental neighbors learn that "beauty on the inside matters more than beauty on the outside."

Little Yellow Pear Tomatoes
Demian Elainé Yumei/Nicole Tamarin, ISBN 0-9740190-2-X
Ponder the never-ending circle of life through the eyes of a young girl, who marvels at all the energy and collaboration it takes to grow yellow pear tomatoes.

Something Special
Terri Cohlene/Doug Keith, ISBN 0-9740190-1-1
A curious little frog finds a mysterious gift outside his home near the castle moat. It's *Something Special*...What can it be?

We Share One World
Jane E. Hoffelt/Marty Husted, ISBN 0-9701907-8-6
Wherever we live—whether we work in the fields, the waterways, the mountains or the cities—all people and creatures share one world.

The Tree
Dana Lyons/David Danioth, ISBN 0-9701907-1-9
Sounding an urgent call to preserve our fragile environment, *The Tree* reminds us that hope for a brighter future lies in our own hands.

Your Father Forever
Travis Griffith/Raquel Abreu, ISBN 0-9740190-3-8
A devoted father promises to guide, protect and respect his beloved children. Transcending the boundaries of culture and time, this is the perfect expression of a parent's universal love.

To view our whole collection visit **www.illumin.com**

Whatever you vividly imagine, earnestly desire,
and enthusiastically act upon must inevitably come to pass.

Jody Bergsma